P9-BZJ-439

To Millie,
Dream Big!
David Ira Rottenberg

Gwendolyn, the Graceful Pig

written by David Ira Rottenberg

illustrated by Lesley Anderson

*For Avery, Koller and Maya—*D.I.R.

*For Mom and Dad—*L.A.

Cedar Crest Books
Natick, MA USA
www.cedarcrestbooks.com

Gwendolyn, the Graceful Pig
by David Ira Rottenberg

Copyright © 2008 David Ira Rottenberg
ALL RIGHTS RESERVED

Cover and interior artwork Copyright © 2008 Lesley Anderson

All rights reserved. No part of this publication may be reproduced, stored in a retrieval system or transmitted in any form by any means electronic, mechanical, photocopying, recording or otherwise, except brief extracts for the purpose of review, without permission of the publisher and copyright owner.

Fourth Printing, 2016
ISBN: 978-0-910291-03-3

Production Date: March 2016. Printed by Everbest Printing (Guangzhou, China), Co. Ltd Job/Batch # 803122

Meet Gwendolyn.

She lives on a farm. Next to the farm is an old fire station. The famous ballet teacher, Natasha Levertov, turned the fire station into a dance studio.

Every day, Gwendolyn gazes in the window at the children learning to dance.

"Oh, how I would love to dance," she sighs. But she's afraid she can't dance because, well, Gwendolyn is a pig.

Gwendolyn has a friend.

Meet Omar.
He's a pig who wants to play football.

But Omar bumps into things and trips. The football coach, Paul "Pug" Potowski, says Omar can't join the team because he's too clumsy.

Omar likes Gwendolyn and thinks she's just about perfect...

...even though she can't dance.

And Gwendolyn thinks Omar is a hug muffin...

...even though he's a little clumsy.

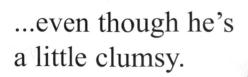

One day, Natasha, the famous ballet teacher, spots Gwendolyn peering in the studio window.

Natasha does not like anyone watching who could be *dancing*.

She motions to Gwendolyn and says, "Come in, my dear, come in! I vill teach you how to learn ze dance."

Natasha says "vill" instead of "will" and "ze" instead of "the" because she is from Russia and has a Russian accent.

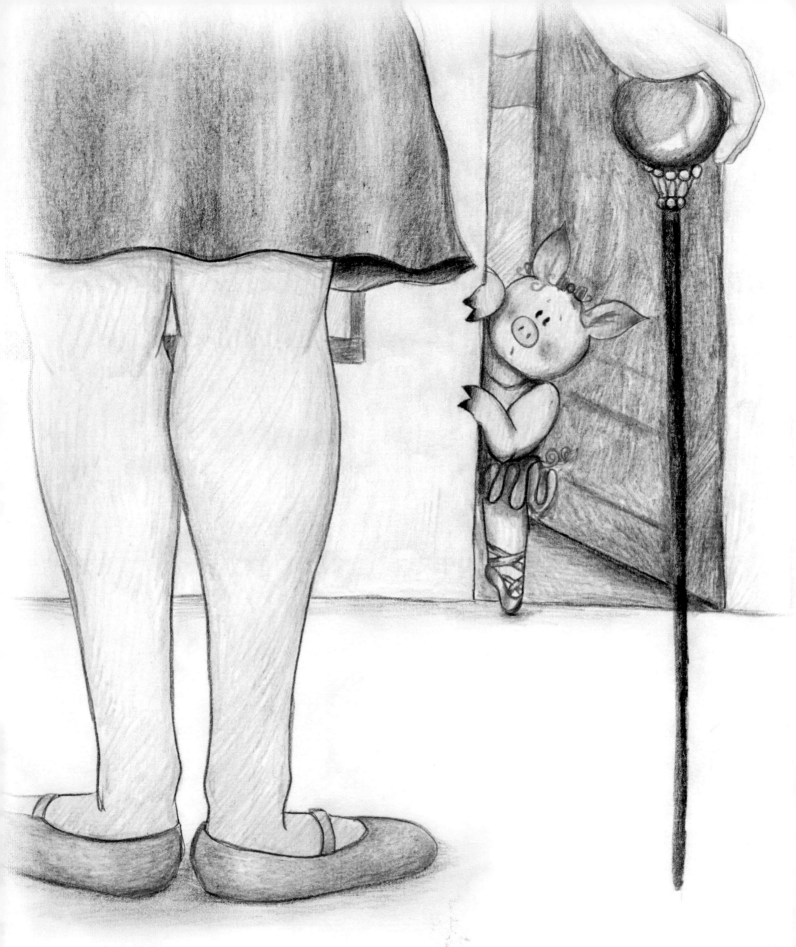

Gwendolyn is very timid, but she pokes her head in and asks Natasha, "Can you really teach me how to dance?"

"Of Course!"
Natasha proclaims.
"I am Natasha
Levertov, ze greatest
teacher of dance in *ze
vorld.* I could teach a
pig to dance!"

Meekly, Gwendolyn says, "I *am* a pig."
Natasha says, "I know. Zat's vhy I said it."

"By ze vay," Natasha asks, pointing to the window where Omar now stands. "Who's zat pig in ze football uniform?"

"That's Omar," answers Gwendolyn.

"Vhy isn't he playing football?" asks Natasha.
"Because," Gwendolyn says, "the coach
thinks he's too clumsy."

"Clumsy?!" Natasha roars. "*No one* is clumsy!
I vill teach him ze dance.
Zen, ve vill show ze coach
who can play football.
Come here, Omar."

Shyly, Omar steps into the studio.

"Omar," Natasha orders. "Step in ze line with Gwendolyn."

Natasha is stern and commanding, but she is also kind and wise.

First, her students bend and stretch to prepare their muscles.

Next, they practice their steps.

Sometimes, they dance s-l-o-w-l-y.

Sometimes,
they dance fast!

Sometimes, Natasha shows them exactly how to move.

Sometimes, Natasha lets them be silly and dance however they want.

Gradually, Gwendolyn and Omar learn to dance.

Omar stops bumping into things,
which makes the girls happy
because he often bumps
into them.

And he rarely trips and
falls on his face,
which makes Omar happy.

As for Gwendolyn, she arabesques, plies, and pirouettes almost as gracefully as the girls!

Natasha is very proud. Even though she boasted she could teach a pig to dance, inside she doubted.

Now she knows without question that she, Natasha Levertov, is the greatest teacher of dance in *ze vorld*!

WORLD'S GREATEST DANCE TEACHER

Then, one day, Omar doesn't come to class. "Vere is Omar?" Natasha demands.

"He's playing football!" Gwendolyn says. "Coach Potowski saw him running so quickly and smoothly, the coach invited him to join the team."

Hearing of Omar's success, everyone in class applauds.
They know how much Omar wants to play football.

"He is not giving up ze dance!" Natasha says in alarm.
"Oh, no," Gwendolyn replies.

"Omar loves to dance...

...*and* play football."

On Monday and Wednesday, Omar practices football,
and on Tuesday and Thursday, he dances.

On Friday, everyone in class, including Natasha Levertov, the greatest teacher of dance in *ze vorld*, goes to the football stadium to root Omar on.

Coach Potowski sends Omar in on defense near the end of the game.

 ?! When the ball is snapped, Omar charges.

 The quarterback sees an enormous pig heading toward him and drops the ball.

Omar falls on the ball.

The whistle blows.
The game is over!

Coach Potowski whoops, "We win!"
Cheers burst from the stands.

The next day is Gwendolyn's ballet recital.

Imagine the excitement when the audience sees Gwendolyn in a bright purple tutu!

She dances with such skill and beauty, everyone gasps in astonishment.

Omar and Gwendolyn do one dance together.

The audience stands
and shouts,

"BRAVO!"

"BRAVO!"

Natasha Levertov becomes even more famous. TV, newspaper and magazine reporters besiege her for interviews—not that Natasha minds.

Gwendolyn and Omar make so much progress,
Natasha awards them special medals...